# David McKee

# Further adventures of KING ROLLO

KING ROLLO and the dishes
KING ROLLO and the balloons
KING ROLLO and King Frank
KING ROLLO and the search

SPARROW BOOKS

Also available in Sparrow Books by David McKee

*The Adventures of King Rollo*
*Now Now, Bernard*
*Tusk Tusk*

Published by Arrow Books. An imprint of the Hutchinson Publishing Group
London Melbourne Sydney Auckland Wellington Johannesburg
and agencies throughout the world.
KING ROLLO AND THE DISHES and KING ROLLO AND THE BALLOONS
first published by Andersen Press 1980. KING ROLLO AND KING FRANK
and KING ROLLO AND THE SEARCH first published by Andersen Press 1981.
Sparrow edition 1983. All rights reserved.
© David McKee 1980 & 1981. Printed in Italy by Grafiche AZ, Verona.

ISBN 0 09 931200 X

# KING ROLLO

## and the
## dishes

"That was delicious," said King Rollo after dinner.

"Yes, really delicious," said the magician.

"In fact we'll wash up for you as a treat," King Rollo said to Cook.

King Rollo and the magician carried the dishes into the kitchen.

"Wash them up by magic," King Rollo
said to the magician.

"That would be cheating. Cook doesn't
use magic," said the magician.

"All right, I'll wash and you wipe,"
said King Rollo.

He washed the first plate.

Then he washed the second plate. It was going to be a slow job.

"Not even a little magic?" King Rollo asked hopefully.

"Cook doesn't use magic," sighed the magician.

"All right, you wash and I'll wipe," said King Rollo.

The magician washed a plate and passed it to King Rollo.

King Rollo dropped the plate and it smashed on the floor.

"Now look what you've done," King Rollo and the magician said together.

"Ssh," said the magician. "Cook is coming."

Quickly the magician made a magic spell.

At once the plate was mended and dry.

The magician looked at the rest of the dirty dishes.

He made another magic spell.

At once all the dishes were clean and dry.

Then Cook came in.

"Well done," she said. "You've washed them just as quickly as I could have."

"But of course," she added, "there were two of you."

# KING ROLLO

## and the

## balloons

King Rollo was looking in his drawer.

He found a packet with three balloons.

"Help me blow up a balloon," he asked Cook.

"Not now," said Cook. "I have to make a cup of tea."

"Help me blow up a balloon," he asked the magician.

"Not now," said the magician. "I have to make a cup of tea vanish."

King Rollo tried to blow up a balloon. It was very hard.

But at last he did it. It was a long green balloon.

Just when King Rollo had the balloon blown up, he let it go.

The balloon flew all over the room.

King Rollo liked that and he did it again.

This time the balloon flew out of the window.

King Rollo blew up the blue balloon.

Then he pulled the neck of the balloon and it squeaked and squealed as the air escaped.

King Rollo blew up the blue balloon again and tied it up.

Then he blew up the last balloon, the yellow one.

In the kitchen the magician made a piece of pie vanish.

Then he wondered if he could make a cake disappear.

Suddenly there was a loud BANG!

Cook and the magician rushed to King Rollo.

"What was that bang?" the magician asked.

"Oh I was just practising some magic," said King Rollo.

"Magic? What magic?" asked the magician.

"I can make a balloon vanish," said King Rollo.

# KING ROLLO
## and
## King Frank

King Rollo was not happy.

"King Frank is coming to tea and I don't like King Frank," he said.

"Why not?" asked the magician.

"He's bossy and he cheats and he's bigger than me," said King Rollo.

"Why did you ask him to tea?" asked the magician.

"Well, nobody else could come," said King Rollo.

"Perhaps he thinks the same about you," said the magician.

"Perhaps he had nobody else to have tea with."

Just then the door bell rang.

"Hello, King Frank," said King Rollo as he let King Frank in.

They took a bat and ball into King Rollo's room.

Then they closed the door behind them.

Later they came out and got a card game.

They went back into the room.

Next they came out for the chess set.

Again they went into the room and closed the door.

After a while King Rollo came out and spoke to Cook about tea.

Cook took their tea into them.

It was a long time before they came out again.

This time it was for King Frank to go home.

"That was fun, he's coming again to-morrow," said King Rollo.

"I thought he was bossy and cheated," said the magician.

"Of course not," said King Rollo. "He's very nice, he's my friend."

Then he added, "But he is taller than me."

# KING ROLLO
## and the
## search

"What are you doing?" King Rollo asked the magician.

"Looking for something," said the magician.

"What are you looking for?" asked Queen Gwen.

"That's the trouble, I can't remember," said the magician.

"We'll help you," said King Rollo and he started to search.

"Pity we don't know what we are looking for," said Queen Gwen.

"Is it this pen?" asked King Rollo.

"No," said the magician.

"Is it these grapes?" asked Queen Gwen.

"No," said the magician taking one.

"This penknife?" asked King Rollo.

"No, but thank you, I did wonder where that was," said the magician.

"If it's your glasses you're wearing them," said Queen Gwen.
"I can see that," said the magician.

"Hamlet the cat?" asked King Rollo.
"Ha, ha, ha," laughed the magician.

"Make a spell to find it," said Queen Gwen. "I could if I only knew what it was," said the magician.

"Make a spell to remember," said King Rollo. "What a good idea," said the magician

"Now I can't remember the spell to remember," he said. "Where is my book of spells?"

"You're sitting on it," said Queen Gwen. "You're sitting on it," said King Rollo.

The magician opened the book and read.

Then he made the remembering spell.

"Has it worked?" asked King Rollo. "Have you remembered what you were looking for?"

"Ah, mmm, yes," said the magician.

"Well, come on, what was it?" asked King Rollo.

"Mmm, the book of spells," said the magician.

Other books in the
Sparrow/Andersen Press picture book series: